Skate the Line

BLUE DEVILS HOCKEY #2

S.J. SYLVIS

For the best man I've ever known.
This one is for you, Grandpa.
I love you. <3

In loving memory of Charles "Dan" Watkins
June 17th, 1937-November 2nd, 2024

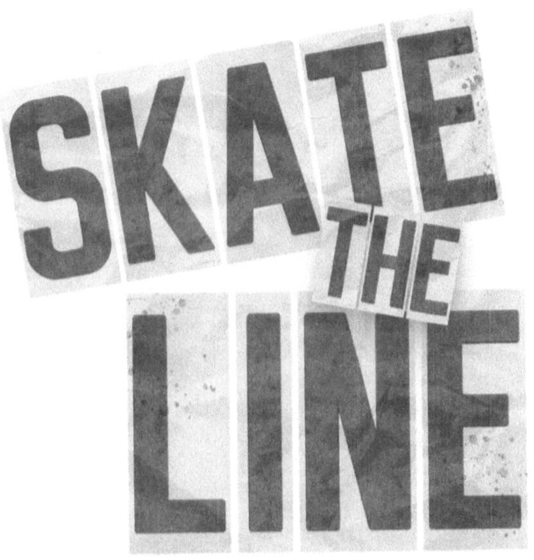

USA TODAY BESTSELLING AUTHOR

S.J. SYLVIS

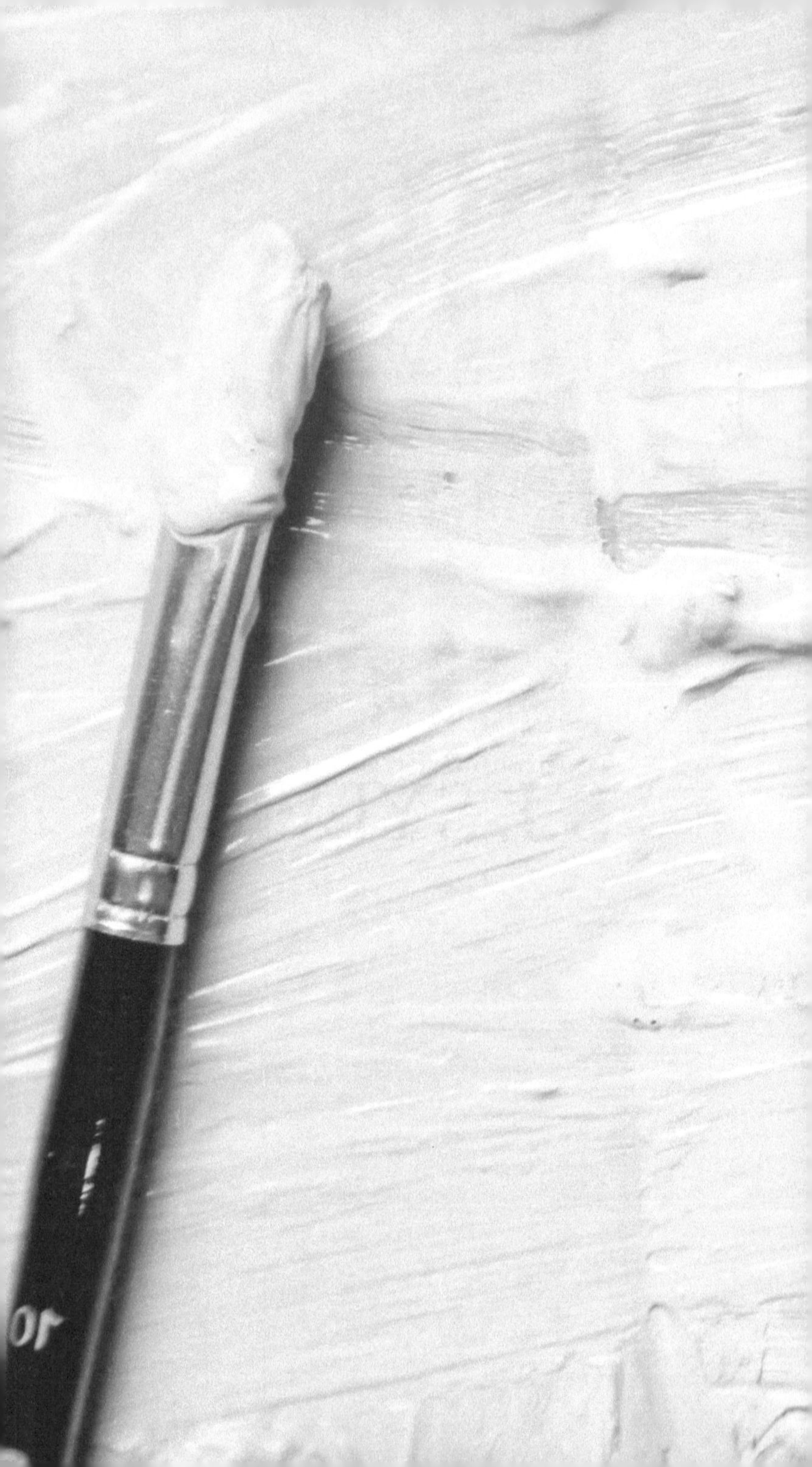

One

SUNNY

"SAY IT WITH ME." The woman's voice calms me. I find myself nodding. "This is the start of the most soul-nourishing year of my life."

I repeat her. "This is the start of the most soul-nourishing year of my life."

A deep breath escapes my mouth as if I'm blowing all my worries away. I slowly peel my eyes open and stare at the crashing waves. The taste of salty water lands on the tip of my tongue, and the ocean breeze wisps at the tendrils of hair hanging from my messy braid.

"This is the start of the most soul-nourishing year of my life," I say again because, just maybe, if I continue saying it and nodding along, I'll actually manifest it into the universe.

I snort and rip an earbud from my ear.

The podcaster continues on, but I find myself focusing on the sounds of the sea instead. I bury my toes into the sand and try to ground myself. I have to get used to my new normal, but no matter how far my feet dig into the granules, something feels off.

The ringing inside my ear pulls me back to reality, cutting off the self-help podcast. I slip my other earbud back in place and answer Ruby's ringtone.

"Hello?"

"Hey, surfer girl."

I roll my eyes. I've been in California for three days, and she's already calling me surfer girl.

"What's u—" She pauses. "Where the hell are you? Sounds like you're standing in the middle of a hurricane."

I unbury my feet and sit cross-legged on a blanket. "I'm at the beach."

"*Ohhhh*," she drags the word out with jealousy. "That's right. I forgot. My bestie is just out there living her best life at the beach."

I laugh sarcastically. "Yep. I'm just out here living the dream. All alone on the beach with a self-help podcast in my ear and nothing but a quickly depleting bank account to my name."

"That's exactly why I called you."

I pick up a seashell and observe the tiny cracks along the edge. "Did my nana bribe you to call me and tell me to go back home?"

Ruby pauses. "She did call me but only to have me check on you."

I knew it. My nana told me to "spread my wings and follow my dreams," but she knows that something isn't quite right. I can't fool her, and I think we both know that my sudden departure from Washington has nothing to do with following my dreams.

"That's not why I'm calling, though. I have a job opportunity."

My heart goes out with the tide. "Ruby," I warn.

She cuts me off. "Hear me out."

Ruby and I are best friends. We don't have that we-grew-up-with-each-other friendship, considering we've only known one another for a few years, but she knows me better than anyone. We met through TEN: The Elite Nanny agency.

It's an elite, privately owned nanny placement agency dedicated to high-profile athletes and their families. The pay is exceptional, and once you're placed with the right family, it's a dream job. I've traveled, gotten free vacations, Christmas bonuses, and I've gained life-long friendships, like with Ruby. I've gained some trauma too, but never mind that.

I throw the broken seashell into the ocean and sigh into the phone. "Fine. What's your job proposition?"

Ruby is well-aware that I've closed a chapter on Washington and with TEN, so I'm interested to hear what this so-called job could be.

"Well, you know TEN?"

I give the phone a strange look. "You mean the nanny agency where we met? No. I've never heard of it."

Ruby ignores my sarcasm. "They've opened up another agency. It's a branch of TEN."

I quickly shake my head. "No."

"You promised you'd hear me out."

I laugh. "I didn't promise you anything."

She pauses, and through the beachy breeze and crashing waves, I hear her soften her tone toward Marybella. "You're supposed to be in bed, monkey."

"Oh, looks like you have to go," I say, knowing it's well after bedtime for Marybella—the little girl she nannies.

"Don't you dare hang up the phone, Sunny."

I roll my eyes and wait on the other end while she gives Marybella three loud smooches and tucks her back in.

"Okay, real quick before she gets out of bed again with some silly excuse for needing water or something."

I smile to myself, remembering when Atlas used to do the same to me when I'd have to stay overnight.

"I'm listening," I say.

"Jillian opened up another branch of TEN. It's called The Nanny Roster. It's exclusive to the eastern part of the United States."

I swallow and remain quiet.

"Word travels with the rich and famous, and apparently, there is a major need for nannies in other parts of the United States—or so Jillian says."

"I..." I grab another seashell and start to rub its smooth surface. "I can't nanny again, Ruby. It's too much..."—*fear*—"drama."

"Chicago is far from Washington."

"Chicago?" The word barely squeezes out of my mouth. "What's in Chicago other than...Oprah?"

Ruby laughs, and I feel my lips turning upward at the sound. "Chicago Blue Devils, Sunny. Get with it!"

My spine straightens. "Hockey?" *Absolutely not.*

"They don't play against each other. I already checked."

I know my sports, especially hockey.

"Unless *they* both make it to the playoffs," I counter.

She scoffs. "As if the Hawks are going to make it to the playoffs. They haven't won a single game."

"There is still time left in the season." My hands shake.

"True." Ruby's sigh cuts through the sound of waves. "Hey, I didn't call to get you out of sorts. I just thought since it was halfway across the country, you might consider it. Especially because Chicago is *artsy*."

"Artsy?" I already know that one of the best art schools is in Chicago, but I'd love to hear Ruby come up with some explanation on what makes it *artsy*. "How so?"

Ruby clicks her tongue. "I don't know...there's, like, museums and shit."

I laugh loudly, and it causes a flock of seagulls to fly away.

"That's right up your alley! Come on!" she pleads. "You don't belong on a sunny beach in California."

I scoff. "What do you mean I don't belong on a sunny beach? My *name* is Sunny."

"Shit, you have a point," she says.

I can almost picture her walking through the kitchen while nibbling on her thumbnail as she tries to think of another solution to get me back to myself. I haven't been the Sunny she knows in months. Not since I left Washington. But maybe even a little before that too.

"Will you at least think about it? That's what you're doing out there in California, right? *Thinking.*"

"I like to call it soul-searching." It sounds better.

"Do you know what's good for the soul?" she asks.

"If you say penis..."

She snorts. "That's obviously implied but not what I was referring to."

"Well, then what?"

"The Windy City, baby!" I wince at her volume.

I shake my head and smile. "Have you ever been to Chicago?"

There's silence.

"No...but I'd have a reason to go if you were there."

"Well..." I pop up from the sand and brush myself off. "Keep looking for reasons, because my answer is no."

Two

RHODES

WHAT THE HELL IS THIS? An escort service?

I stare at the screen with an angry brow while a bead of sweat rolls down my back. I reread the text from the team's manager, making sure our signals aren't crossed. The nanny agency even sounds like an escort business—*The Nanny Roster.*

Is it a list of nannies that we can hire to watch our children...or is it a list of nannies that we can hire for other things?

It sounds a little suspicious.

Or maybe I'm just on edge because I'm at my wits' end with the endless number of nannies I've been through lately.

Ellie is a good kid. I know it's not her that is the issue here.

It's the women I keep hiring.

Or if you ask them, it's *me*. I'm the problem.

I sigh, and it sounds like a growl.

Malaki walks into the media room where we watch film tapes, but apparently, it's doubling as a hang-out room today. He plops down onto the couch and opens a Gatorade. He gulps it as loud as humanly possible, clearly trying to get my attention, just like my five-year-old daughter would do.

I slowly raise my gaze above my laptop screen and glare at him. "Can I help you?"

"Nope." He throws his empty Gatorade bottle into the trash halfway across the room and winks after making it. "But I can help you."

"Doubtful."

Out of all my teammates, Malaki is the one who makes the most jokes about fucking Ellie's nannies, and it irritates me because the entire reason most of them leave is because I *won't* fuck them.

After looking at The Nanny Roster logo again, I pull my attention back to Malaki. I have no idea why he's so early. I'm the only one who shows up hours before team practice to hone my skills in silence, but given that my choices are limited and he's taking up space, I throw him a bone.

I spin my laptop around, and he gets this excited look on his face, like he's eager to please me.

"What does this website look like to you?" I ask.

Malaki pops up from the couch with too much energy and stalks over to the table. He's still got that *you're-asking-me-for-advice* look on his face, but I don't comment on it because, yeah, I'm perplexed by it too.

"Well…" He rubs his chin as he peers down at the screen. "My first thought?" he asks. "They're hot as hell."

My shoulders tense, and my lips flatten.

"But"—he raises his palm—"the website looks too professional to be what I want it to be."

"Which is?" I already know the answer.

"My pick of the litter." He wiggles his eyebrows.

I quickly spin the computer around with irritation. "So

you think it looks like an escort service too?" A tight breath leaves my chest. "Fucking figures," I mutter.

Why can't there be some older, married woman listed that is looking for something to fill her time now that her own children are grown? Someone who would be good with Ellie but also someone I won't find naked in my shower, waiting for me? Or someone I won't have to worry will climb into my bed late at night, wearing nothing but some scandalous piece of fabric that she begs for me to peel from her body?

Why is that so hard?

I'm asking for too much. That's why it's slim pickings. But I don't have another choice—I'm a single father without even a fucking second cousin nearby to help.

Malaki leans his elbows onto the table. "I never said it looked like an escort service. I mean, it'd be legit if it were some type of dating site, but again..." He comes around the table and stands over my shoulder. "It's too professional looking."

After a few beats of silence, he speaks up again. "Did Kevin send that over? Trying to help you find a nanny?"

I nod. "It's a new nanny service made strictly for pro athletes."

"And given you can't keep a nanny satisfied, he sent it to you," a voice says from behind.

I peer over my shoulder and glare at Kane. He's one of our rowdier and younger teammates.

"You make it sound like I give in and fuck them, and then they aren't pleased."

"We all wish you'd fuck them. Maybe you'd get that stick out of your ass if you did."

I slam my laptop shut, and by the time I turn around, Kane is already halfway through the door and heading to the locker room.

Malaki chuckles. "I love it when you two bicker. It's like foreplay before practice."

Another scowl, and suddenly, Malaki is on his way to the locker room too.

They're just as annoying as my nanny situation.

I pull open my phone and linger on the photo of Ellie on my home screen. She's blowing a bubble with her pink bubblegum, and although our fans consider me to be cold, a bit standoffish, and too focused at times, if there's anyone who can thaw my hardened heart, it's her.

I click on Dylan's name—one of my more mature teammates—and type a text.

> Me: Hey, man. Can you do me a favor and ask Angela if she's heard of this nanny service? Kevin sent it over, and I'm not sure if it's reputable or not.

He texts back a moment later.

> Dylan: Having nanny problems again?

> Me: Fuck off.

> Dylan: I just sent her the link. I'll let you know what she finds out.

I toss my phone aside and head to practice. Maybe a quick puck to someone's face will ease my mood.

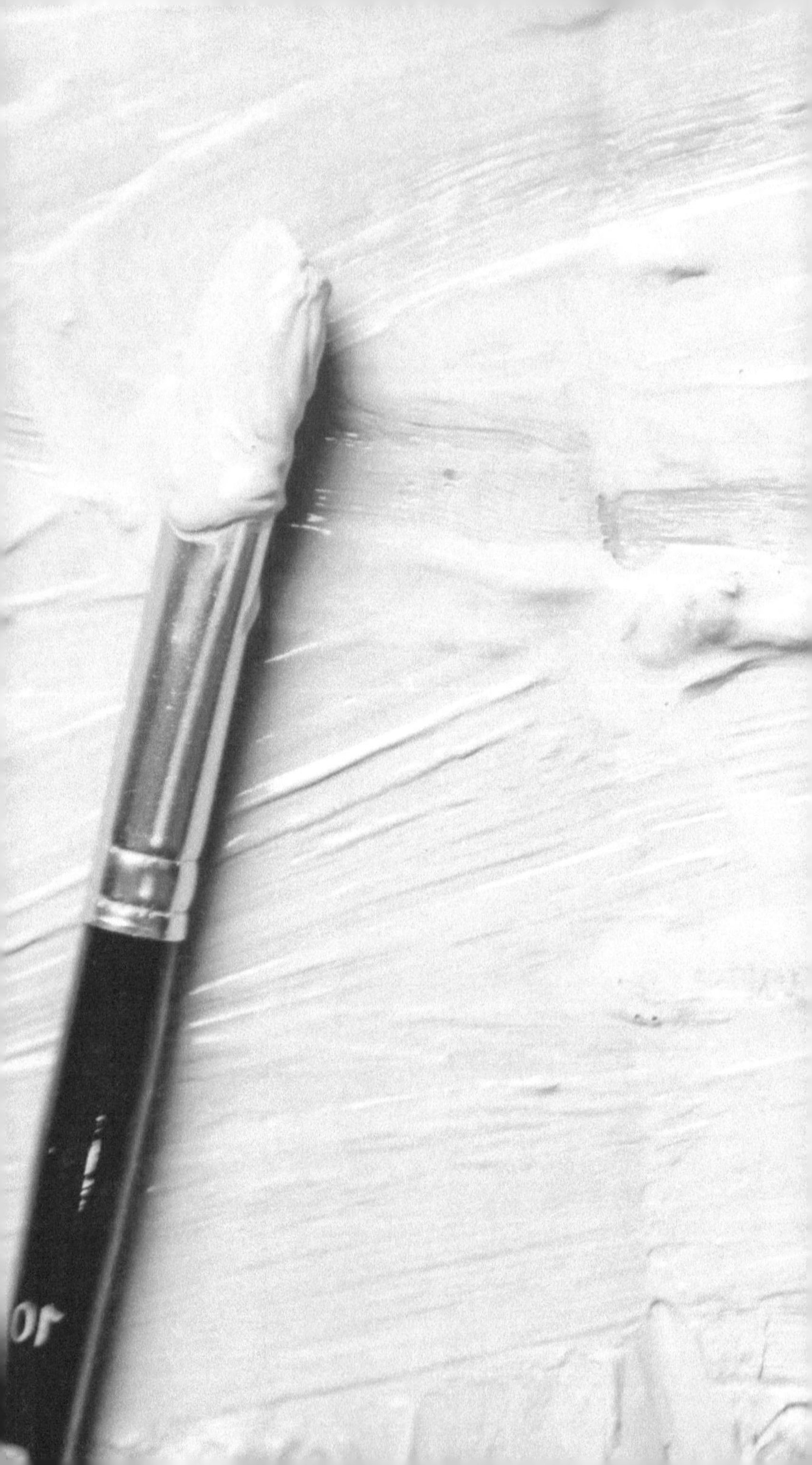

Three

SUNNY

THE MOOD IS SET.

The ambience is giving vibes, and although I feel every bit of crazy, I'm here for it.

Shuffling cards fill the empty space between me and a woman who looks like she could double as a Harry Potter character. The smell of lavender is overpowering enough to mix in with the salty air of the ocean just outside the purple curtains.

"I'm feeling sunshine from you," Celeste muses.

She has a little twinkle in her eye that I'm pretty sure I'm just imagining.

"Well, my name is Allison, but I go by Sunny." I smile, and she mirrors me.

"That makes sense."

She shuffles some more cards and takes a deep breath while closing her eyes. Purple eyeshadow shimmers underneath the filtered sunlight from above, and when she opens her eyes again, she starts pulling cards left and right.

My phone vibrates, but I ignore it. Instead, I stare at Celeste's long maroon fingernails filtering through the tarot cards falling from her hands.

"Ah," she singsongs.

I scan the cards she's straightening in between us.

I have no idea what they mean. Up until about twenty minutes ago, I didn't even believe in this sort of thing.

But if the universe could give me a sign, *one single sign,* to direct me on the right path, I'll believe anything at this point.

"You've pulled quite a lot of cards, Allison."

I wish she wouldn't call me that.

"Is that bad?" I ask.

"You're the only one who can decide that."

That's not an answer. That's a riddle. And to be honest, I don't appreciate it.

Celeste taps her fingers on the table before landing on the card with a sun in the center surrounded by light blues and grassy lands.

"This is very fitting. You are a light, meaning you attract goodness. You have beauty inside of you, and you're willing to spread that around to others. I sense that you'll attract success going forward. Your energy attracts good people."

"Not always," I mutter.

Celeste doesn't pry. She circles the next card and stares at me from across the table. My phone vibrates again, and we both look at it.

I see three texts from Ruby, all of which are facts about Chicago.

She's been sending me facts for two days now.

Chicago has the second-largest public transportation system. It has more than 450 million bus and train rides, meaning you won't even need a car!

Chicago has more than 60 art museums! Right up your alley.

*Chicago is home to one of the best art schools in the country—
you could go back to school!*

"This one"—the tapping of Celeste's fingernail pulls me
back to her reading—"is called The Fool."

That doesn't sound good.

Her smile catches me off guard. "It means new beginnings.
Maybe you'll be taking a risk soon? Making a change?"

She slides another tarot card beside it, and I freeze. "The
Lovers."

I choke on air. I did not come here for relationship advice.
That is the last thing I want to think about as I contemplate
becoming a nanny again for another pro hockey player.

Wait. Contemplate?

Am I really contemplating it?

According to my dwindling bank account, I am.

"Relax, Allison. It doesn't always refer to romantic relationships."

Can she read minds?

"The Lovers card means that you're being led to love, but
it can be a friendship, family, even a pet. It just means that you
have love coming to you in the future."

I'm skeptical. I bet she tells everyone that they're being led
to love.

Still, I point to the two cards that resemble one another.
"What are those?"

"Oh. This is interesting. You've pulled both The Emperor
and The Empress. The Emperor means a new job opportunity
may be presenting itself, but it also comes with stability. You'll
have the power to make your own rules and set boundaries
within your new role."

A quiet, sarcastic noise slips out.

I should have set boundaries at my last job.

"The Empress is very similar as it also means new beginnings. Would you consider yourself to be creative?"

A small smile touches my lips. "Yes."

It's been so long since I've been able to sit and lose myself in front of a canvas.

Celeste raises an eyebrow. "The Empress is typically pulled for those with creative abilities. She also demonstrates a nurturing soul."

The more the tarot reader explains the cards, the more I start to second-guess the reading. It's sounding very much like Ruby called this woman and told her what to tell me to get me to go to Chicago.

New beginnings, new job opportunities, setting boundaries, and creative abilities...

"And that one?" I nod to the last card.

The shimmer on Celeste's eyelids catches the sun again with her narrowed gaze. "That is The Hanged Man." Her blue eyes pierce me, and I'm not sure if she's meaning to be intense, but she looks serious. "It means sacrifice. Whether that be in your future or your past. Maybe you've had to make a sacrifice recently, or you'll have to make one eventually."

I clear my throat as a distraction. Just this morning, Ruby made that exact comment to me—that I've had to sacrifice so much as of late. My home, my sense of self, my future, my outlook on men and relationships, and worst of all, my own judgment.

Celeste grabs me by the hand. It startles me, even though her touch is soft and warm. "The good thing that comes with The Hanged Man is wisdom. If you're recalling a sacrifice in your life, then take comfort in knowing you've been through the trials already. Trust your intuition, sweet child. Let your energy lead you. Trust yourself in whatever your future holds."

My phone vibrates again. I'd bet my life it's another text from Ruby.

Celeste eventually releases my hand, and my session

finishes. It's donation only, and I tip her more than I planned on, but I would be lying if I said my outlook wasn't a little skewed afterward. There's a weird energy flowing through my body that I swear wasn't there before.

I slip out from the purple curtains and step onto the sidewalk blanketed in sand. I shake out my hands as I make my way to the shade and finally open my texts.

It's a photo of Ruby and me in our bikinis from last summer. The only off thing about the photo is that the background isn't the pool that I know should be there. Instead, it's a cityscape that is *clearly* photoshopped in. There's a billboard behind us that says *The future awaits*.

It wouldn't surprise me if Ruby edited that into the photo too, but I can't help but question if the universe really is giving me a sign.

I glance back to the purple curtains and reread the cardboard sign: *Free Tarot Readings— Donations appreciated!*

My heart beats with a little bit of anticipation as I type.

Me: If I ask for more information about this hockey player you think I'd be a good nanny for, will you stop sending me facts about Chicago every hour? Also, you suck at Photoshop.

Ruby: Jillian already bought your ticket. You leave tomorrow.

Her face pops up on the screen with an incoming call a second later.

I roll my eyes.

Chicago, here I come.

Four

RHODES

"THANK SCOTTIE FOR ME,"—*AGAIN*—I say to our goalie, Emory.

He brushes me off as he heads toward his car. This is his first season with the Blue Devils, but he's made a name for himself, and he's made a name for this team too.

Not to mention, his wife has saved my ass multiple times. Whenever I have a situation with a nanny, she steps in and takes care of Ellie for me. It's not her responsibility, though, and every single fucking time a nanny *"goes to the bathroom"* and doesn't come back during one of my games, my anger rises to unfathomable levels.

I glance at Ellie's rosy cheeks. It's not often I let emotions cloud my judgment or alter my thoughts, but *damn.* There's a pang of sadness lingering in the back of my mind when I glance at my daughter.

My mom said that my endless nanny situation is affecting Ellie, and I practically told her to fuck off in the politest way I could think of.

But she's right.

Every time a nanny leaves my daughter high and dry, the wound digs deeper.

"Where do you think Laken went?" Ellie innocently asks.

She grabs onto my hand, and we walk in the direction of my truck. I try to think of a good reason for the disappearing act of her new nanny that she'll actually believe, but she isn't stupid. Ellie is smarter than most kids her age—at least according to her kindergarten teacher.

Last week, I had my first parent-teacher conference. I was prepared for a rundown on Ellie's grades and maybe a few examples of how well she writes her name, but instead, what I got was a fucking intervention.

Ellie's education isn't our concern, Mr. Volkova. It's her social and emotional development.

I sat in that tiny-ass chair while her teacher and Mrs. Honor, the guidance counselor, reamed me with question after question regarding Ellie's life outside of school. They wanted to know what her schedule was like, if there was stability in her life—particularly since I'm away a lot of the time due to my hockey schedule—how she handles not having a mother figure in her life, if she does age-appropriate activities...

To top it all off, they implied that Ellie attending my games on a school night surrounded by rowdy fans, most tipsy on alcohol, isn't age appropriate.

They weren't wrong, but what I wanted to say was *fuck off.*

I'm doing the best I can.

I'm a single father who has a rigorous work schedule who can't keep a nanny happy for more than one week at this point.

"Did you finish your homework?" I ask Ellie, ignoring her question about our recent runaway.

I catch her weary look in the rearview. "I don't have homework, Daddy. I'm in kindergarten."

Ah, right.

"I knew that." I turn the truck on and play it cool. "I was just trying to catch you in a lie."

Ellie crosses her arms and pouts. "I don't lie to you."

I grin. "I know."

By the time we make it home, Ellie has fallen asleep. I know I should probably wake her up and get her in the bath or, at the very least, brush her hair, but after the game I just played, I'm near exhaustion.

Parenting is a full-time job, and I never expected I'd have to do it alone.

I never expected to be a parent in the first place.

When the court reached out and informed me that I may be the father of Ellie, I assumed there was a mix-up. After learning that it was Gia who had passed, recognizing her as a one-night stand, I willingly took a paternity test. I was always careful when it came to sex, especially with puck bunnies, so there was no chance the baby was mine.

But then, my life flipped upside down.

Considering that Gia didn't really have a family of her own—none of whom could potentially gain custody of an infant, at least—it was up to me.

Now, here I am, a single father to a five-year-old girl who doesn't have a mother. I'm not resentful, and I'm glad Gia put me on the birth certificate, though I wish she would have told me beforehand so I could have had at least an ounce of preparation. Regardless of all that, it gave me Ellie.

I exhale deeply after shutting Ellie's bedroom door.

I head to the kitchen and open the fridge to snag one of the premade meals that Emory has introduced me to. High in protein, no mess, and they taste alright. Good enough for me.

As soon as I pop it into the microwave, my phone buzzes

with an alert that only sounds when someone is on the property.

My hackles rise.

The door is always locked.

After having Ellie and becoming fully responsible for someone who is as helpless as it gets, my defensive abilities grew sharper. You don't know protectiveness until you have a daughter.

I pull up the camera, and my shoulders tense.

You've got to be fucking kidding me.

My blood pressure rises with each stride toward the front door. I swing it open before she can even raise a fist.

"Did you get lost?" I snap, leaning my shoulder against the doorjamb. "Kidnapped? Tricked into getting into a van with hockey players willing to let you suck their dick?"

Laken's cheeks turn red. She gasps with surprise, and I deepen my glare.

"Don't act surprised, Laken. You tried to suck mine on day one."

It's true. I found her on her knees in my bathroom one evening after I stepped out of the shower. I gave her a warning and emphasized that it was her *only* warning. Sure, it was after I mumbled *"shlyuha"* under my breath, but unless she knew fluent Russian, she had no idea that I'd called her a whore.

"I forgot my things," she mutters.

She refuses to meet my eye. I have the urge to grip her chin and *make* her look at me so she can see how angry I am that she left my daughter all alone at my hockey game just hours before, but the last thing I want to do is give her a reason to start any bullshit with the media.

"Seems you forgot my daughter too," I jab.

"I..."

I interrupt her by pushing off the doorjamb and standing tall. "Leave my property."

Her jaw slacks.

Before I push the door shut, I give her one more warning —something I said I wouldn't do. *One and done* when it comes to me.

"If I ever see you around my daughter again, I'll have a restraining order put on you."

"Are you kidd—"

The door latches, and the lock clicks.

I set the alarm and head toward the kitchen for my dinner.

Three bites in and I'm opening my laptop. I type the words *The Nanny Roster* into the search engine because I truly have no other option.

Five

SUNNY

I TAKE a sip of my latte and stare out the window of my new-for-now home. I'm smack-dab in the middle of the busy Chicago city with skyscrapers as my neighbors. Last week I was surrounded by easygoing SoCal people and salty air. Today, I'm watching business men storm to and from a sleek building with too many windows to count.

"How's the view?" Ruby asks through our video call. She's wearing a princess crown and has purple eyeshadow up to her forehead.

I roll my lips to suppress my laughter while I watch a tiny hand move in the frame as it applies bright-pink blush to Ruby's cheeks. Ruby is completely unbothered by the fact that she looks like a clown.

"The view is as beautiful as the makeup Marybella is applying to your face. Good job, Mary!" I say.

Ruby flutters her eyelashes. "So beautiful."

We both laugh and continue on with our conversation while Marybella adds sparkles.

"Have you looked him up yet?" Ruby asks.

I glance out the window again. Chicago is busier than anywhere else I've lived before, but if what Ruby says is true about Rhodes Volkova, then I think I can manage the bustling city for a little while—at least until I get on my feet.

Rhodes Volkova isn't your typical pro hockey player. He has the stats of a veteran, but every article states that he's gruff, standoffish, and fully immersed in the game of hockey. One article noted him having a daughter and being a single father but nothing specific about what happened to her mother. His life is private, which could be good or bad, depending on how you look at it. Another article focused on how attractive he is and labeled him as the most desirable bachelor in the league. However, considering how private he is, who's to say he isn't in a relationship?

I take another sip of my latte and nod at Ruby.

"And?"

I shrug. "You were right. He's...private."

"You mean, he's not an arrogant man who parades women—"

My eyes widen. I shake my head, mouthing for her to shut up. Ruby slams her lips together and glances above the screen of the phone. "You know what, Marybella? I bet I would look *fabulous* with some jewelry. Why don't you go find some to match my crown?"

Marybella gasps. "You wight! I be wight back!"

"I'll be right here waiting!" she calls out.

Ruby, with her face covered in makeup, pops back into the frame and continues on with our conversation. "He's clearly not a manwhore, right? He's rarely seen with a woman, and word has it that he's desperate for a nanny that won't pull any puck bunny bullshit with him."

I give her a look. "Where did you hear that from?"

"Jason and Kelly."

"You're getting your gossip from Marybella's parents? I thought it was Jillian!" *Oh god.*

"Relax!" Ruby retorts. "It's both. Jillian told me that Rhodes specifically asked for someone who wouldn't crawl into his bed and ask him to..."—she lowers her voice—"fuck them."

My latte flies from my mouth. I cough and sputter so hard Ruby asks if she should call 911.

"Sorry." I cough again. "I just wasn't expecting you to say that."

Marybella is back with what looks like twenty necklaces. In between her placing them over Ruby's head, she keeps talking. "I know, but the first person that came to Jillian's mind was you, and I couldn't agree more. It's the perfect job for you. A grumpy single dad who openly admits he doesn't want a..."—she takes a pause—"relationship."

I nibble on my lip. It seems Rhodes Volkova and I have that in common.

Ruby keeps selling me on the idea, hence why I'm in Chicago.

"I also heard that he can't keep a nanny for more than a couple of weeks because they.... Well..." I can tell she is contemplating her choice of words. "Let's just say he has to fire them for not respecting his wishes."

Interesting.

"And..."

The plot thickens. "And what?"

"And I was told that he's so grumpy with some of the nannies that they just end up not coming back."

"Grumpy," I repeat.

Grumpy I can deal with. It's the charming ones you have to watch out for.

A shaky breath clambers from my mouth as I reach for my

laptop. "It all sounds too good to be true." I exit out of the website for The Chicago Art Institute and type The Nanny Roster.

Ruby shrugs. "Maybe he's gay."

"What does that mean?" Marybella asks.

Ruby freezes. "That's out of my paygrade. Ask your parents."

I stuff down a laugh, and Ruby moves on quickly.

"Anyway, where is my optimistic Sunny at? I'm the pessimistic friend in this friendship. You're the optimistic one."

My lips lift into a smile while I continue searching the nanny website. My finger hovers over one of the potential nannies listed.

"Ruby." My tone lowers. "Did you put me on the website?!"

Her eyes grow so big I can hardly see the sparkles that Marybella applied.

"Ruby!" I shout. "This is just like that stupid dating app you put me on!" I slam the laptop shut and glare at her through the phone. "We both know how well that worked out!"

"Oh, look at the time. I gotta go!"

I cover my face with my hands. "I'm trying to stay on the down-low! Remember?"

"I didn't put your picture up! Not to mention, why would anyone from Washington be looking on The Nanny Roster's website? They don't even know it exists."

I groan. "I'm hanging up so I can panic in peace."

Before she hangs up the phone, she says, "If Jillian calls you, answer! Or else you'll be in Chicago without a job."

I remove my hands to roll my eyes at her, but she's already hung up.

As if on cue, my phone rings, and Jillian's name flashes on the screen.

Fate? Is that you?

If so, fuck off.

Six

RHODES

"I CAN ASSURE you the women we hire are highly professional, Mr. Volkova. I personally know each one and can vouch for them. Out of the many years I've run a nanny business, I have rarely had any complaints."

I grunt. "Meaning you've had complaints."

The woman on the other end of the phone pauses. There's a sigh, and I raise an eyebrow. I click through the list of nannies for the hundredth time while I wait for her to form some misleading response to my obvious dig.

"I wouldn't necessarily call them complaints. In order to respect the privacy of my employees, I will just say that if there were any complaints, they did not come from the clients. They came from the nannies themselves, which forced me to drop a client or place the nanny elsewhere due to their wishes."

What the fuck does that mean?

After a few seconds of heavy silence, she clears her throat. "Are there any that you are interested in? Do you have any questions? Would you like to set up an interview with any of the women?"

Not really, no.

"I'm still looking."

And I'm slowly running out of time.

"I have one that I think will be a good fit for you."

I lean back in my chair and rap my knuckles on my counter. I say nothing and thankfully the woman, Jillian, means business, because she jumps right to it.

"I just sent a link to her profile to your email."

I've already clicked the link by the time she starts her spiel.

"She's one of my more private employees. She doesn't like to be in the spotlight, which should be perfect considering one of your stipulations is that your daughter stays away from the media."

I nod to myself.

"She's in her mid-twenties, but she's very mature. She's from Washington and used to work for my other nanny agency out there. There has never been a complaint from any of the clients she's worked with."

"Is she married?" I ask.

It's unlikely, but a man can hope.

Jillian clears throat. "Um, no. But if you're suggesting that she'd—"

"I am," I interrupt. "I want to know if she's the type of woman who will try to climb into bed with me."

She laughs, and it throws me off. I know I sound like a cocky asshole, but when you've been burned so many times, you've gotta ask these sorts of questions.

"Mr. Volkova, listen. I know you've been through the wringer with some of your past nannies. I've heard it from you, your manager, and the gossip. I don't know the ins and outs of what has happened in the past, but I can assure you that Sunny Edwards is *not* that type of woman. That's why I'm suggesting her to you."

I click on her profile. *No picture?* Does that mean she's ugly? All the other nannies have their photos posted above their bio.

"Is she a lesbian?" I ask.

There's a loud gasp on the other end of the phone. "The sexual preferences of my employees are none of your business."

I hum under my breath. "I disagree."

A beep comes in through the line, and I see that Ellie's school is calling. I mumble a curse.

"Fine," I snap. "Set up an interview. Email me with the details. I have to go."

After hanging up on Jillian, I answer the number that I *really* hate to see on my screen.

"Hello?"

"Mr. Volkova, hello. This is Principal Kelley."

"Is Ellie okay?" I stand up from my kitchen island. I begin looking for my keys because from the sound of Principal Kelley's voice, I know something is up.

"Ellie is fine, but we are having a behavioral issue today."

Fucking fantastic. I lift up the pile of construction paper on the kitchen table, sending glitter flying into the air and all over my shirt.

"Okay?"

Where the fuck are my keys?

In the middle of searching for my keys and holding the phone up to my ear, I rip my shirt off and throw it toward the living room. Glitter is everywhere. Ellie's markers roll onto the floor. I bend down to pick them up and quickly swipe my keys that are somehow under the table.

"She won't stop speaking in Russian."

God damnit, Ellie.

It's not funny. It really isn't.

But it's never, "*Wow, your daughter is bilingual!*" It's always, "*Can you please tell her to stop speaking in a foreign language?*"

"Put her on the phone," I say.

The principal sighs. "Yes, sir."

Ellie's childish voice hits my year. "Privet?"

"Ellie."

"Chto?" she says innocently.

This is what we're doing now?

"Tebe skuchno?" I ask her if she's bored in Russian, and I like to state the fact that my voice is nowhere near as playful as hers.

My Russian isn't the smoothest now that I rarely speak it. My father was the one who mostly spoke the language, but after his quick departure from my and my mother's life, I abruptly stopped. When I turned eighteen, I added an A to Volkov, just for one more final *fuck you* to him.

However, my clever daughter *loves* to use the language ever since my mother sent her old Russian translating tapes, hoping that Ellie will at least speak the language.

I'm still cursing her.

Ellie doesn't answer me, and I smirk.

"Not so clever now, are you?" I ask. "Why are you speaking Russian when you know very well that neither your teacher nor any of your classmates know the language? Are you that bored, Printsessa?"

That is the *only* term I use in Russian. The first time I laid eyes on her, some hidden part of me emerged, and I whispered the word under my breath. It's stayed ever since.

"Da."

I roll my eyes at her response.

"If you don't stop, you won't be going to my game this weekend."

I swear I can hear her pout through the phone.

"Fine. I'll stop, Daddy," she relents.

Ellie has me wrapped around her finger, but she knows when I'm serious and when she's able to push my buttons a little further. Right now, I'm fully fed up, and it has a lot to do with my nanny situation and less about her behavior.

"And I want you to apologize to your teacher"—my tone deepens—"in English."

Her little sigh makes my lips twitch. "Okay."

"I'll see you after school. I love you."

"I love you too."

Principal Kelley comes back onto the phone, and I pinch the bridge of my nose, knowing she's judging the hell out of me.

"Thank you, Mr. Volkova," she says. "I'm sorry to have bothered you, but it seems she really only responds to you."

Ellie has trust issues, just like me.

"It's not a problem. I apologize that this behavior is occurring."

I'm doing the best I can.

"Ellie speaking Russian isn't troublesome behavior. It's just inconvenient. She isn't a bad kid."

"I know she isn't," I say as monotoned as it gets. "We will work on her attention-seeking behavior."

Part of me wants to reprimand the principal and her teacher for not stimulating her enough in class to keep her occupied, but I know it isn't the real problem.

After getting off the phone with the principal, I down the rest of my coffee and quickly type a text to Jillian.

> Me: I'll be at Chicago Bakes in thirty. Tell Ms. Edwards that if she wants a well-paying job, to meet me there. I won't wait if she is late.

Tell her to keep her legs closed too.